BAD Nana

THAT'S SNOW BUSINESS!

*for Bertie Duckworth,
whose mum is the
baddest I know!
X X X*

First published in Great Britain by
HarperCollins *Children's Books* in 2019
HarperCollins *Children's Books* is a division of HarperCollins*Publishers* Ltd,
HarperCollins Publishers
1 London Bridge Street
London SE1 9GF

The HarperCollins website address is:
www.harpercollins.co.uk

1

Text and illustrations copyright © Sophy Henn 2019
All rights reserved.

ISBN 978–0–00–826813–8

Sophy Henn asserts the moral right to be identified
as the author and illustrator of the work.

Typeset in New Clarendon 14/22pt by Goldy Broad
Printed and bound in China by RR Donnelley APS

BAD Nana

That's Snow Business!

Sophy Henn

HarperCollins *Children's Books*

CONTENTS

Hello!

My name is
Jeanie and I am still 7 ¾.
I STILL like badges,
but I also like patches too,
and my NEW pencil case
and guinea pigs in HATS.
But I've gone off milkshakes because
my friend Wilf told me a joke when I was
drinking one, and I laughed so much
some came OUT of my nose.
They haven't tasted the same since.

Oh, and I reeeeeeaaaaaalllllllllllllyy
like SNOW. I mean, who doesn't?

I have a little brother called Jack, who has been going through an annoying phase his ENTIRE LIFE, and it doesn't look like this is going to change any time soon – WORST LUCK. My mum and dad say we have to keep him, so I have had to rise above it and be a better person and set a good example.

Which is NOT HARD as he is SO COMPLETELY awful.

We all live together in a house in a town. Sometimes the house feels quite BIG and sometimes it feels very SMALL.

My friend Marcy has two houses on account of her mum and dad NOT getting on quite as well as they thought they would. I can see this as both good and bad. GOOD because you get two bedrooms, BAD because you have to remember to take EVERYTHING you need each time

you change houses.
And BAD because all
your brothers and
sisters are with
you whichever
house you are
at anyway. At
least that's
what I reckon

SUKEY

– I didn't ask Marcy because she isn't too
keen on talking about it at the moment.

Our other friends are called Wilf and
Sukey. Wilf's house is above a shop, which
is exciting, and Sukey moved houses to
one that's miles and MILES away.
But I am actually going to visit her soon,
Mum said, and I CAN'T sleep a wink
because I am soooo excited.

As well as **friends**,
I ALSO have some **family**,
and I don't just mean my mum and dad
and **annoying** brother.

I have quite a bit of **other** family
all over the place, but **lucky** for me
my **favourite** bit of family lives only
eight minutes and thirty-six seconds
away, if you get a **wiggle** on,
and it's called . . .

BAD NANA.

BAD NANA isn't BAD in the **normal** way, like a FILM BADDIE

or an OLDEN-DAYS BADDIE

or a
DINOSAUR
BADDIE.

She's **more** FUN than that, and she only gets up to NO GOOD if someone makes her absolutely have to, at least that's how it happens MOST of the time. And, anyway, things just seem to be much MORE fun and definitely MORE exciting when she is around.

And she has a pet. I really, really, REALLY want a pet. Jack does TOO. It is the only thing in the whole wide world that we actually agree on (other than mushrooms – they are WRONG). Only Dad WON'T let us have one because he says he and Mum will end up looking after it. I tried to point out that pets are

scientifically proven to **reduce STRESS** and, as he and Mum seemed to be stressed pretty much ALL THE TIME, looking after a pet could be just what they need. This made him go a funny colour, and Mum told me to go upstairs. I am pretty hopeful, though, because you just can't argue with SCIENCE.

Anyway, because Jack and I spend SO much time at **BAD NANA'S** house, it is like we sort of have a pet. A part-time pet. A sometimes-but-not-always pet called *Liberace*, and he is an EXTREMELY fluffy pink cat. I know cats aren't normally pink, and I'm almost certain that this would NOT normally be *Liberace*'s natural colouring.

I know this because I had to help **BAD NANA** wash him after he had an accident with a tin of sardines (also WRONG), and the water went a bit pink when we rinsed him.

We also discovered that he is MAINLY fur and NOT MUCH cat. Which probably explains why he was trying to get into those sardines in the first place.

BAD NANA does tend to fancy things up like that, though. And she's always saying how she needs a bit of twinkle about the place. I think this explains all the sparkles around her house and her ginormous earrings. And her sparkly turban. And the trunk of shiny sequinny clothes she has in her room that we dress up in sometimes. I asked BAD NANA why she had them, and she said they were from when she worked in show business. That's one of the things I love about BAD NANA – she's done all sorts of things and they come in handy every now and again. Like when she REPAIRED the car using an old pair of tights and some hair grips (from when she was in the SAS), or knew all the capital cities for my homework (from when she was a JET PILOT), just all sorts of things, really. Anyway, it turns out her show-business skills came in handy again, well, sort of. At least they did until it all went a bit WRONG . . .

SECOND

Snow WaY

It was ACTUALLY Jack who noticed the poster when he was on his way out of BEAVERS at the town hall, which was super a n n o y i n g because then he acted like it was all HIS idea, which of course it wasn't because he never has ANY ideas, let alone good ones. Anyway, it was a poster for the WINTER WONDERLAND VARIETY SHOW that was going to be happening in the town hall in less

26

than a WEEK. It was TOO exciting.
Firstly, because it was happening so
QUICKLY there was just no time for it
to get boring. Secondly, because our
town had NEVER had a WINTER WONDERLAND
VARIETY SHOW before and, thirdly, because
EVERYONE was invited to audition for
it. I wasn't sure what a variety show was,
but I was sure I wanted to be in it. What
with all her show-business experience,
BAD NANA knew and she explained that it
was all different kinds of acts gathered
together in ONE BIG SHOW, a bit like the
big tins of different types of chocolates
you get on special occasions. Well, this
just made it all the MORE exciting,
except I REALLY hoped I wasn't going to
be the coffee cream.

UGH.

The actual show was going to be in our town hall and up on the STAGE with the swishy red curtains, which we are NEVER allowed on normally because the grown-ups think we are all idiots and would immediately fall off. AND there were going to be lights AND microphones and maybe EVEN a smoke machine. Mrs Valentine from the town committee was going to organise it, which I thought was an excellent idea as, although I didn't know her in the slightest, I DID know she had bright-pink hair, which felt like the right type of hair colour for show business.

I told Marcy and Wilf about the WINTER
WONDERLAND VARIETY SHOW first thing
when I got to school the next day, and we
all agreed that we **completely** HAD
to audition for it as they hadn't been
allowed up on to the stage with the swishy
red curtains either. We had also somehow
missed out on parts in the nativity play

at school. We didn't **even** get picked to be **stars**, and Barry Bates got a part as a star and he **sing-shouts**. So we felt like the WINTER WONDERLAND VARIETY SHOW might be our chance to SHINE. Like **stars**. Just NOT nativity-play stars.

We hit a bit of a **problem** early on as after a very long THINK we all agreed that **showy talents** were NOT our strong point, and we couldn't come up with a **single** thing we could do that would get us a SPOT in the show. Unluckily, Georgina **overheard** us talking and starting HOOTING. It turns out this was her version of laughing, and the reason she was laughing was because she thought we were all a bunch of UNTALENTED losers and had NO **chance** of being in the show.

I realise this sounds **extremely cruel** and MEAN, and it actually is, but Georgina does this sort of thing all the time, especially to me, so I am very nearly used to it by now. It always makes me feel a little bit **wibbly**, though, no matter how much I know it SHOULDN'T.

Then to make everything a **million** times WORSE Georgina used *her* showy talents to T$_A$P D$_A$N$_C$E away, singing about the sun coming out tomorrow. But just for a CHANGE Georgina was completely WRONG, because there was NO sun tomorrow.

Instead there was
absolutely masses
and masses
and BUCKETS
and BUCKETS
of . . .

...SNOW!

It was so **completely brilliant** and **pretty** and FANTASTIC that me and Jack accidentally **played** snowball fights **together** before breakfast. I am not sure we have ever played outside BEFORE **breakfast** or even TOGETHER, but that's **snow** for you. At school all anyone could talk about was **snow** THIS and **snow** THAT, and it was half **brilliant** and half **puddle-y**, what with everyone's

outdoor stuff hanging up and drying out all over the place. It wasn't until lunchtime that Marcy, Wilf and me remembered that we still had NO showy talents for the WINTER WONDERLAND VARIETY SHOW, and the clock was ticking. Then I suddenly realised we had a *SECRET S*P*A*R*KLY* WEAPON, someone who knew all about razzle dazzle, showbiz and ALL THAT JAZZ and that someone was . . .

. . . BAD NANA.

Lucky for us, **BAD NANA** had some great ideas for talents for Marcy, Wilf and me. Some seemed to be a bit more DANGEROUS than others, and Mum put her foot down about sawing one of us in HALF, but in the end we all decided on a very sparkly, good old SONG 'N' DANCE routine.

Super annoyingly, MUM also put her foot down about Jack being part of the very sparkly, good old SONG 'N' DANCE routine too. I tried to explain that he couldn't possibly take part because he COULDN'T sing OR dance OR do ANYTHING except be really annoying. But she wasn't listening and somehow Jack was ALREADY dressed head to toe in sequins, so it didn't really seem to matter what I thought.

We were all SO excited that we were going to have some showy talents for the show, and BAD NANA seemed to be super excited TOO. The snow had completely NOT stopped snowing AT ALL and Mr Meakins, the school caretaker, hadn't been able to shovel it away *FAST* enough because there is only ONE of him for Pete's sake, so the next day was in actual fact a . . . SNOW DAY! This was perfect as it

meant we had **extra time** to PRACTISE our act for the audition that afternoon. We all walked round to **BAD NANA'S**, and after she had unstuck Jack's tongue from an icicle we got to work. **BAD NANA** really put us through our *PACES*, and if it hadn't been for the constant supply of biscuits I am NOT at all sure we would have made it through!

As we all got ready to go to the audition, Marcy, Wilf and me were so excited and all agreed we had already been on quite the journey, starting at three people (plus Jack), who could NOT at all do a very sparkly good old song 'n' dance routine, and ending up at three people (plus Jack), who could very nearly almost do a very sparkly, good old SONG 'N' DANCE routine. We also agreed we'd had much TOO MUCH fun while we were practising to get sad if we WEREN'T picked to be in the WINTER WONDERLAND VARIETY SHOW. And, anyway, BAD NANA had promised us extra-special hot chocolates with ALL the trimmings as a REWARD for our hard work, so really we had won already.

We were waiting by the door for **BAD NANA**, which was already weird as usually it's the other way round, when suddenly the *SLIDING DOORS* to the kitchen opened and a super-duper, extra-BRIGHT and completely DAZZLING light burst out. And then suddenly it was gone and there was **BAD NANA** in her BIG coat. I had no idea what had just happened, and I thought it was most probably aliens, but then **BAD NANA** told us all to get a wiggle on (which was a bit RICH) and we all left for the town hall.

Once we arrived at the town hall it was **pandemonium**. It felt like the WHOLE town was there, being talented, all over the place. You could SMELL the **excitement** and I'm not **completely** sure it was a **nice** smell. **BAD NANA** walked over to Mrs Valentine, who was quite easy to **spot** on account of her **hair**, but was looking a bit PANICKY and like she didn't **really** know what to do.

BAD NANA had a jolly good rummage in her handbag and produced one of those really, really LOUD air horns, which was *quite* a surprise. Then she said it was in there from the football, which was *even* more surprising. Anyway, when it went OFF everyone suddenly STOPPED being talented and FROZE, like surprised musical statues, and BAD NANA handed it to Mrs Valentine, smiled and we all got in a line.

Just as soon as Mrs Valentine had explained to us that this was just a bit of fun and she would try to INCLUDE as MANY acts as possible and she hoped we would all enjoy ourselves because it really was just a bit of fun, the double doors of the town hall were FLUNG OPEN and there was Bobby Trulove.

Bobby Trulove is the closest thing our town has got to an actual FAMOUS PERSON. Apparently he used to tread the boards, which BAD NANA said means he used to be on the stage. But NOT the stage with the swishy red curtains in our town hall (though I bet he's ALLOWED), but BIG, proper, fancy STAGES in BIG, proper, fancy PLACES.

In fact, Bobby Trulove was SO famous he was *even* in panto with Sir Ian McKellen – well, that's what BAD NANA said, and apart from the fact that she hardly ever lies, she is also friends with Bobby, so she SHOULD know. In fact, they are very, very old and very, VERY sparkly friends because BAD NANA told me they used to give it the old razzle dazzle on the cruise ships back in the good OLD days, which I think mainly involved a LOT of sequins and even more showing off – on WATER.

Anyway, it was always good fun if Bobby came to visit because he and BAD NANA would dress up and sing songs and do old-people dancing, which is like NORMAL dancing but just a bit more careful.

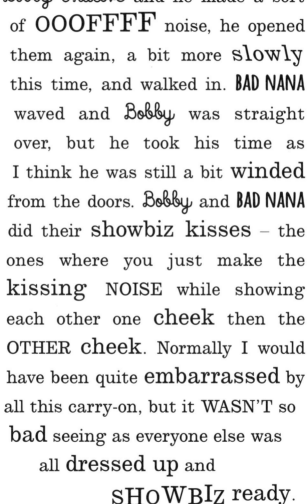

After the double doors had flung back into Bobby Trulove and he made a sort of OOOFFFF noise, he opened them again, a bit more slowly this time, and walked in. BAD NANA waved and Bobby was straight over, but he took his time as I think he was still a bit winded from the doors. Bobby and BAD NANA did their showbiz kisses – the ones where you just make the kissing NOISE while showing each other one cheek then the OTHER cheek. Normally I would have been quite embarrassed by all this carry-on, but it WASN'T so bad seeing as everyone else was all dressed up and SHOWBIZ ready.

BAD NANA asked Bobby what he was doing here, and Bobby's face went all tight and he did a **weird** LAUGH and said he thought he would just pop in and see how it was all going. Then he raised ONE of his eyebrows, just one, and said he might ask **BAD NANA** what *she* was doing here too, and then her face went all tight and she said she was just here to support us, and then Bobby said oh, that's nice and his face went EVEN tighter, and then he asked **BAD NANA** why was she wearing her BIG coat and if she didn't take it off now she wouldn't feel the **benefit** later, and **BAD NANA'S** face went even tighter and she said OOOH, this old thing? I FORGOT I was even wearing it, but wasn't a sequin BOW TIE a bit snazzy just to see how something was going? And Bobby said Hmmmmmm. And I KNEW something was going on.

But I had no idea WHAT.

First on the STAGE was the almost brand-new ~~Hooper Dooper~~ dance troupe, who didn't really dance, but did hulahooping. I liked it a LOT. They had even put tinsel in their hair, as an EXTRA showbiz touch. They were all EXTREMELY smiley, even when they

were hula-hooping round their **necks**, which looked like it must really **hurt**, and other than one <small>small</small> CATASTROPHE, when a hoop FLEW OFF the top of Miss Dobson from the library, it went REALLY well and everyone in the queue couldn't help but give them a **very BIG** round of applause.

Second onstage was Mrs Wiggins from the chemist's. She looked ever so pretty, but got a little flustered and said sorry and then got off the stage again, which I thought was a real SHAME, but show business ISN'T for everyone.

Third was actually Mr Pickles and Pepé, which sounds like TWO people, or at least ONE person and a dog. But it ISN'T. It's Pepé, who lives on BAD NANA'S road, and a puppet called Mr Pickles. To be fair, Mr Pickles is a very fancy puppet and he sits on Pepé's knee while Pepé does the voice for him WITHOUT moving his lips at all, but moving Mr Pickles's instead, so it's like Mr Pickles is ACTUALLY talking. Anyway, they were very funny and Mr Pickles even sang a song while Pepé drank a glass of water. Sort of.

After that there was Mr Whittaker from the newsagent's very impressive BIRD whistles ... Penny Heard's DOUBLE recordering using only her NOSE ... A VERY dramatic Shakespeare play by Mr Roberts, Jack's English teacher, where he played ALL the parts ...

And then there was Georgina dressed in one of her many princess dresses and acting all shy and giggly, which didn't

fool ME for one single second. She sang a sort of DISCO-ish *SPEEDED-UP* version of one of those princess songs, and seemed to be doing one of her modern-dance routines too. I couldn't be sure about the dancing as her dress completely covered her legs, but you could tell they were moving about a LOT, and then she finished with a kick/splits combo, which even I had to admit was SPECTACULAR.

Marcy, Wilf and me agreed that our WHOLE town was actually really surprisingly TALENTED and Mrs Valentine looked very pleased indeed, and while this was GREAT, it was also quite a lot more nervous-making as this meant we had to be EXTRA good if we were going to make it into the WINTER WONDERLAND VARIETY SHOW.

FINALLY it was **our** turn, and after we'd **found** Jack in the cupboard in the kitchen (no one knew why he was in there, not **even** Jack) we got up on the STAGE with the swishy red curtains and **unsurprisingly** DIDN'T immediately fall off it. BAD NANA gave us all a w𝗂n𝗄 and Bobby gave us the DOUBLE thumbs up. Suddenly the music was playing and we were off . . .

I am NOT sure at what point it started to get a bit muddled, but I DO know that we DIDN'T *quite* end up in the finishing pose we had practised, though we *were* wearing our finishing FACES that BAD NANA had taught us. It hadn't gone as well as in some of our practices, but we'd definitely given it ALL of our per cents and you CAN'T really DO any more than that.

As we were walking off the stage, I noticed **BAD NANA** wandering on to it, wearing her big-eyed wibbly old-lady smile and my tummy did a little flip as I knew something was about to happen. Mrs Valentine smiled at **BAD NANA** and asked if she was okay and if she wanted a go, in that way people sometimes use when they talk to old people, like they are very deaf babies. **BAD NANA** opened her

eyes and looked all surprised, like she had never *even* thought of the idea, and then suddenly yelled, "HIT IT!" to no one in particular and dropped her BIG coat. Suddenly the dazzling light was back and I realised that it HADN'T been aliens at **BAD NANA'S** earlier, but had in fact been **BAD NANA**. Well, **BAD NANA** and about a BILLION sequins.

This was all VERY surprising and got even more surprising when BAD NANA started to sing about there being NO business like SHOW business and dancing around with her walking stick, which she seemed to be using half for dancing and half for propping herself up after she'd just done a bit of dancing.

Liberace even appeared out of BAD NANA'S tartan trolley, adding to an already quite dazzling performance.

Part out of surprise and part out of relief that she'd got to the END without hurting herself, and part out of it actually being really very good, the whole hall clapped and cheered once BAD NANA had finished her act. BAD NANA was BOWING and enjoying her applause. Well, I say "bowing" – it was

more of a **bob** and **nod** really – but she
was DEFINITELY enjoying herself.

Well, it had been QUITE the ten minutes, what with OUR performance and then **BAD NANA'S** surprise performance, and I wondered what on earth was going to happen next. Then I didn't need

to wonder any more, because just as BAD NANA left the stage Bobby Trulove arrived on it *FASTER* than I have ever seen him move before and removed his kagoul to reveal a sequin JACKET to match his sequin BOW TIE. My eyes started to hurt and I wished I'd brought my sunglasses, then I realised why showbiz people wore theirs ALL the time – because of the sequin dazzle, OBVIOUSLY.

Suddenly Bobby started COUNTING very loudly, which I thought was quite odd, but when he EVENTUALLY got to four he started to sing all about razzle-dazzling people. Unlike BAD NANA, Bobby didn't have a stick to use for his dancing, but he did *LEAN* on the piano every so often when he got worn out.

In a VERY ambitious move that I don't think any of us saw coming, Bobby ended his song by going down on one knee and flinging his arms out. Everyone clapped and cheered and Bobby seemed to be really ENJOYING his applause too, so much that he just stayed there and didn't move an inch, so we sort of kept clapping and he STILL didn't move, and then everyone's hands hurt so the clapping slowed down a bit and he STILL didn't move, but by then we could hear him saying he was STUCK, so Wilf and I helped him up and off the stage.

Well, all this had come as such a HUGE super surprise because **BAD NANA** and *Bobby Trulove* hadn't done their usual careful dancing at all. In fact, they had both been COMPLETELY uncareful. But Marcy, Wilf and me all agreed that **BAD NANA**, *Bobby Trulove* and ALL the sequins had been VERY impressive. After we ALL got off the stage, we went over to see **BAD NANA'S** best friend, *Cynth*, who had been manning the tea urn. She was going to do a turn playing the spoons later on, and I could not think

of a more **perfect** act for someone who
makes so much **tea**!

To CELEBRATE all our performances,
and no one doing themselves an
injury, *Cynth* even broke into the
Women's Institute **biscuit tin**, which
I thought was very brave of *Cynth*
as the WI can be VERY **protective** of
their **biscuits**. (I heard Billy Gibson
sneaked one at BEAVERS and got
caught, and he wouldn't *even* **say**
what happened, but he **swore** he would
NEVER eat a custard cream again.)

Marcy, Wilf and me and Jack were hopping about with all the excitement of the auditions, but BAD NANA and Bobby Trulove were very unusually QUIET and eyed each other suspiciously over the tops of their teacups. Then BAD NANA said she didn't know that Bobby was auditioning and Bobby said he didn't know that she was auditioning, and BAD NANA said it was a spur-of-the-moment-type thing, and Bobby said what, she just happened to

be wearing a billion sequins, and **BAD NANA** said YES, and that they were very insulating against the cold, and Bobby said, pffft, and **BAD NANA** said she didn't think kagouls and sequin jackets were that usual for a weekday, and Bobby said he just fancied a change and I looked at Cynth to see if she knew what was going on, but she just shrugged her shoulders and carried on polishing her spoons.

We stayed to watch the rest of the acts, and **BAD NANA** handed out some disgusting fish-paste sandwiches, and I wondered how someone who gets biscuits so right could get sandwiches so wrong. Then Mrs Valentine thanked everyone for coming along and performing so marvellously, and told us that she would put up the LIST of acts that

would be IN the show on the town-hall **notice board** tomorrow morning as unfortunately she couldn't quite SQUEEZE us ALL into the show. I thought that was a very **nice** way of saying some of us weren't quite up to it, but it didn't bother me one bit as not **everyone** can be RIGHT for **show business**.

The next morning, **BAD NANA** was at our house before I'd even started my second bowl of Choco Pops, but thankfully she wasn't covered in sequins again as I think my eyeballs might have just popped OUT of my head if there had been any dazzling at that time in the morning. We all had our fingers AND toes crossed as the DJ on the radio read out which schools would be CLOSED because of the snow, but it turned out Mr Meakins must have been CONSTANTLY shovelling snow ALL night, for Pete's sake, because our school was NOT read out. WORST LUCK. **BAD NANA** said not to worry but we could walk by the town hall on the way to school to see who was in the show and HURRY UP. Well, this was easier said than done as it seemed the MORE snow there was,

the more CLOTHES
you had to wear.

There was already a crowd round the notice board by the time we arrived at the town hall. Even Marcy was there, but not Wilf as it's not on his way to school. After I had a think about it, I realised it wasn't on the way to school for me either, but BAD NANA seemed EXTREMELY keen to find out WHO was on the list. Marcy ran over and DOUBLE high-fived me immediately, so I knew it was good NEWS. I am not sure exactly why, but somehow Mrs Valentine had decided our very sparkly, good old SONG 'N'

DANCE routine would be in the show. Our finishing faces must have SAVED the day! So now all we had to do was work on the rest of the act and we would be FINE. I turned to tell BAD NANA, but she had already made a beeline for the board and was zooming in on the list when she bumped straight into Bobby Trulove. They gave each other the beady eye and then slowly looked at the board.

I scriggled through the crowd, past **BAD NANA** and Bobby Trulove, and looked up at the board myself and NOT only were Marcy, Wilf and me and Jack in the show but **BAD NANA** AND Bobby Trulove were too! The LIST said so! It was the best news – we were ALL in. I was so excited I turned round and hugged them both. But it turned out they had already walked away, so I was ACTUALLY hugging Miss Dobson and Pepé, which was *quite* a bit embarrassing.

The notice also said that the **first rehearsal** was THAT actual evening, and Marcy and I might have **hopped** a bit with excitement, but then we STOPPED because we saw Georgina **punching** the **air** because she was in the WINTER WONDERLAND VARIETY SHOW too. As we all walked to school, she jogged past us and said **congratulations** on having our COMEDY ACT picked for the show, which was just **mean** because she **knew** it wasn't *supposed* to be **funny**. But I didn't think about it for long because Marcy and I had a **snowball** fight and then we went to find Wilf to tell him the completely **brilliant** news.

After school, I was SO excited about the rehearsal I could *barely* eat seconds of dinner. **BAD NANA** seemed pretty excited too, and was *humming* and wiggling about the WHOLE time. None of us needed our showbiz clothes as it was JUST a rehearsal, which was a HUGE

relief because all those sequins made my eyes hurt. **BAD NANA** DID wear a big black cape, though, AND a sparkly turban, which I thought was a bit OVER THE TOP for the town hall on a school night but I didn't say anything.

It turned out it wasn't just **BAD NANA** who was OVER THE TOP for the town hall, because *Bobby Trulove* was also wearing a cape and a GIANT hat. Or maybe EVERYONE else was just super underdressed, but I didn't think so. The only other person who looked a bit snazzy was TINY Daniel Pauls, who was also wearing a VERY fancy waistcoat over the top of his jumper, but everyone knows magicians HAVE to wear fancy waistcoats, even just for rehearsals. Apparently TINY Daniel Pauls is the world's smallest magician, though he had no ACTUAL proof of that so we just had to take his word for it. But he is extremely SMALL and 3ft 2" is pretty little for being magic.

The rehearsals began and **BAD NANA** immediately volunteered to go **first** and swished up on to the stage before anyone could STOP her. She told everyone, but mainly Mrs Valentine, that whoever **opened** the show should really have had previous **professional** stage experience as it was a HUMONGOUSLY BIG **pressure** because you had to **win** the audience over right then and there, and that she thought maybe THAT person should be— Then, *QUICK AS A FLASH* and with quite a bit of swishing, cape-wise, Bobby Trulove was suddenly onstage and said it should probably DEFINITELY be **him**. Then **BAD NANA** peeked out from under his cape to say it **actually** should really DEFINITELY be **her** and then they carried on *shoving* each other, basically

behaving in the exact way Jack and I do just before we get a HUGE telling-off and possibly even a biscuit BAN. Mrs Valentine even had to use the air horn to make them STOP.

BAD NANA swished to the FRONT of the stage like a GIANT bat and told Mrs Valentine that she really knew about THESE things, what with her stage

experience, and maybe she should actually help out a bit more with the show.

Then Bobby said that she SHOULDN'T trouble herself, not with her hips and, anyway, he had FAR more stage experience and some of his was from THIS actual century and that HE should really help Mrs Valentine.

Then BAD NANA went a bit pink, and Bobby NARROWED his eyes and they started *shoving* each other again, and Mrs Valentine looked a lot like she didn't really want to be there at all.

This went on for a bit because no one really knew what to do, but then finally Marcy suggested that they BOTH help Mrs Valentine, and Mrs Valentine looked relieved and SCARED all at once and said yes. But like it was a question.

Marcy then suggested that maybe the ~~Hooper Doopers~~ should start the show, and I agreed as they were so happy-making, and Wilf thirded the idea and Mrs Valentine looked very happy and said that was a GREAT idea and let's definitely do that.

BAD NANA and Bobby Trulove didn't seem to agree, though, and both went quite a bit pink and SCOWLY and walked off backstage, huffing extremely LOUDLY, so even the ~~Hooper Doopers~~ could hear.

I started to wonder if it might have actually been ALIENS dazzling us at BAD NANA'S the day before, and maybe they HAD taken her and replaced her with someone who was NOT pleased for other people, and did NOT want to have fun, and actually went a little bit NOT very nice where stages and shows and sequins were concerned.

While I was wondering this, **BAD NANA** and *Bobby Trulove* suddenly reappeared from the wings, completely un-huffed, and GRINNING an awful lot as they helpfully sat down next to Mrs Valentine, which was quite the turnaround, mood-wise.

Everyone was VERY excited as the Hooper Doopers all got up onstage and went to find their hoops. I could not WAIT to see them hooping again and had everything crossed that they would keep ALL their hoops on themselves this time!

They had been gone for AAAAAAGES, and you could feel everyone getting slightly LESS excited, except BAD NANA and Bobby, who had started giggling. I was SO happy that they seemed to be getting on again, but I couldn't quite ignore the funny feeling in my tummy. It's WEIRD because my tummy always seems to know before I do when BAD NANA is up to something, and this didn't feel like a good something.

The ~~Hooper Doopers~~ came back onstage looking a bit LESS super and told everyone that they couldn't FIND their hoops, and BAD NANA and Bobby gave each other a wink, which my tummy CONFIRMED WAS SUSPICIOUS.

Then Bobby suggested that they have a
go WITHOUT the hoops and that maybe
the hoops were a bit distracting
anyway and in his experience the BEST
acts didn't really need PROPS and things
to make them entertaining. Well, no
one had expected THAT, especially
NOT the Hooper Doopers, as the hoops
were sort of the whole point of their act
and WITHOUT them they were just a

group of grown-ups wiggling about a bit. But they gave it a go and it turned out they DID just look like a group of grown-ups wiggling about a bit. By the end, Miss Dobson looked SO upset she had to *RUN OFF* the stage and then the others followed, saying they would really rather have hoops and that maybe they weren't *quite* ready for the spotlight after all.

Mrs Valentine then quite firmly suggested Mr Pickles and Pepé have a go at being first even though BAD NANA and Bobby Trulove volunteered. AGAIN. I thought this made a lot of sense and they were both as COMPLETELY brilliant and SLIGHTLY creepy as they had been on audition day. We all clapped when they finished their act and then Bobby casually mentioned that while he felt Mr Pickles had REAL star potential, he didn't really feel that Pepé had the X FACTOR, and he would know, what with ALL his show-business experience, and BAD NANA nodded, looking quite SERIOUS. Well, that made everyone VERY confused, as (while none of us wanted to actually say it *and spoil the illusion*) we all knew quite clearly that WITHOUT Pepé Mr Pickles was just a *slightly* frightening-looking doll. There was a very TENSE silence when I really hoped BAD NANA would say something and tell Bobby Trulove not to be so silly or MEAN or rude, like she normally would, but she DIDN'T.

Then Mr Pickles s i g h e d and said that he couldn't possibly do the act WITHOUT Pepé and this made Pepé smile happily and it also made me think how strange ventriloquist acts are, and then the TWO of them got up and left the hall.

BAD NANA said it was such **BAD** luck they had lost TWO ACTS already, and *Bobby* agreed, but I could tell they weren't **REALLY** sad at all, especially when they **both** got onstage during TINY Daniel

Pauls's **magic** act and ~~swooshed~~ about in their **capes**, which they said **added** DRAMA but actually just meant we couldn't **see** TINY Daniel Pauls or his **magic**. But we **could** hear him CRY.

After all that I was in such a fuddle and everything seemed to be UPSIDE DOWN and my tummy was funnier than ever. BAD NANA and Bobby Trulove were actually being NOT very nice to everyone who got up on the stage and I didn't know why. Normally BAD NANA would tell the person acting like her to knock it off, but without HER to tell HERSELF to knock it off where would it end? Would it even end? Or would it actually carry on forever and ever and for a bit it really felt like it might because . . .

They pulled **funny faces** to make Mr Whittaker LAUGH so he COULDN'T do any **bird whistles** . . . SOMEONE plugged up Penny Heard's **recorders** so she COULDN'T play them both with her **nostrils** and just went a **funny colour** instead . . .

And a wh**OOpe**e cushion *mysteriously* found its way on to the old-fashioned chair and made *quite* a **RUDE noise** at a very **important** part of Mr Roberts's Shakespeare stuff.

One by one each act left the hall, feeling quite a bit embarrassed and NOT at ALL like they wanted to be in the show any more. WINTER WONDERLAND was turning into a WINTER WASTELAND, but BAD NANA and ~~Bobby~~ kept telling Mrs Valentine there was NO NEED to worry as there were LOADS of things they could do to fill in the time, like juggling, or OPERA singing or the ROBOT. And then finally my brain caught up with my tummy and they both AGREED that something

fishy was going on and it WASN'T just the disgusting paste sandwiches. Every time BAD NANA and Bobby Trulove got near the stage with the swishy red curtains they seemed to go a bit razzle-dazzle CRAZY and started acting like Jack does when he has eaten TOO MANY pink wafers. I knew it wasn't actually pink wafers that were making them act this way, though, as Cynth had run out of them hours ago. It was actually quite a relief when the rehearsal was over.

BAd NANa & BObBy TRULoVe?

REALLY?

There was only ONE day left for practising, which might have been EXTREMELY worrying but was in actual fact NOT as there were only FOUR acts left in the WINTER WONDERLAND VARIETY SHOW . . .

Marcy, Wilf and me and Jack and Georgina, BAD NANA and Bobby Trulove, so we had plenty of time to practise. I did worry that there wasn't much variety, though.

Marcy, Wilf and me and Jack and Georgina walked to the town hall after school and you could tell **none** of us was very **excited** to be going to rehearsals after what had happened to all the other acts the day before. Well, all the other acts EXCEPT **BAD NANA** and Bobby Trulove. Georgina didn't even tease me when I fell **face first** into the snow so I knew she must be **really** fed up.

When we arrived at the hall I could also see Mrs Valentine's pink hair hanging down, along with her head, and she looked very, VERY unhappy indeed. Apparently BAD NANA and Bobby Trulove had been there for hours already and they had planned out the whole show and wouldn't listen one tiny bit to ANYTHING Mrs Valentine had to say, even though *her* hair was the MOST showbizzy out of all of everybody's. I tried looking on the bright side and said that as the show was tomorrow it was a good job it was all worked out so everyone would know EXACTLY what was what. And then Mrs Valentine

said something about THAT
not really being a **problem
any more** and went off
to see if there were
ANY pink wafers left.

Marcy, Wilf and me and Jack and even Georgina gathered around the stage just in time to hear the END of a medley of show tunes. I was waving madly at BAD NANA to try to get her attention, but she and Bobby Trulove were both

singing with their eyes **closed**. Once they FINALLY opened their eyes and realised we were all there and waiting, **BAD NANA** and Bobby said we needed to do a run-through, which is show-business talk for a practice.

This all sounded VERY promising, but it didn't take long for them to start going razzle-dazzle CRAZY again. Georgina went first and began to sing her princess song, but her dancing WASN'T *secret* this time as she WASN'T wearing her HUGE princess dress. Unusually, Georgina looked a bit worried and she was RIGHT to look that way because two lines into her song, when she was singing about being sad and alone like princesses do, she DISAPPEARED. Just like that. POOF. Then we heard a yelp and realised that she hadn't ACTUALLY disappeared, but *really* a trapdoor had opened in the stage and she had COMPLETELY fallen through. At first I thought it must have been an accident, but when Bobby Trulove suddenly

appeared singing about putting on a happy face and then **BAD NANA** appeared dressed as a clown I realised it HADN'T been an accident at all.

We *RUSHED* onstage and looked down the hole to see Georgina, who now ACTUALLY did look sad and was a bit alone like one of her song princesses. BAD NANA and Bobby Trulove said they really couldn't see what the fuss was about and that they were only trying to cheer it all up a bit. Then something really, REALLY weird happened, something that has never, EVER happened before . . . *I felt sorry for Georgina* and Georgina even did a little cry and that also NEVER happens. I was so cross with BAD NANA and Bobby Trulove and I was just about to tell them, but before I knew it I was wearing sparkles again and it was time for Marcy, Wilf and me and Jack to practise our very sparkly, good old SONG 'N' DANCE routine.

As we got onstage, Bobby Trulove told us where our MARK was, which is show-business language for the place to STAND at the start. "Our MARK" was actually in quite a surprising place as it was NOT in front of the curtain but behind the curtain, and not the swishy red curtains that open and shut but the

UNswishy ones at the BACK of the stage that do NOT move. Ever.

It turns out they had also decided to CHANGE our song so it was now quite a lot less of a WHOLE song and very much more like singing the chorus to *their* song.

Quite quietly.

I wasn't sure how things could get any worse. But then **BAD NANA** and Bobby Trulove showed us all exactly how and started fighting between themselves . . .

Bobby Trulove let DOWN the tyres on **BAD NANA'S** unicycle,

so **BAD NANA** SWAPPED Bobby Trulove's juggling balls for water balloons . . .

BAD NANA REPLACED the strings of Bobby Trulove's ukelele with liquorice laces

so *Bobby Trulove* bunged up **BAD NANA'S** tuba . . .

But when *Bobby Trulove* greased
BAD NANA'S TAP SHOES

and then **she CUT** the
ELASTIC in his **trousers**

we *knew* things were getting
OUT OF CONTROL.

It was now COMPLETELY impossible NOT to notice that **BAD NANA** and Bobby Trulove had been properly RAZZLE-DAZZLED by the sequins and the spotlights. It was EXTREMELY clear they each wanted the stage with the ~~swishy red curtains~~ ALL to themselves and they didn't seem to care about anyone else, which was so back to front for **BAD NANA** because she is always the person who wants EVERYONE to have fun.

I knew things had gone TOO FAR, but I didn't have a clue what to do about it as normally BAD NANA would have come up with a plan, but things were NOT at all normal. She was *SHOW-OFF*, bossy-boots, RAZZLE-DAZZLE CRAZY and I was in a PROPER pickle as this had NEVER happened before, ever.

I went and got into Jack's cupboard in the hall kitchen and did about TEN MINUTES of really hard thinking, then I realised exactly what I should do and that was have a lemon sherbet and ANOTHER think, but this time I had to think like BAD NANA.

Just as I got to the fizzly sherbety bit in the middle of my lemon sherbet, I got an IDEA – maybe the best IDEA I have ever had – and it really felt like a BAD NANA sort of IDEA, and I went to find the others.

Marcy, Wilf and Jack and even Georgina were all busy looking EXTREMELY miserable at the back of the hall, like a row of *slightly* melty snowmen.

I handed out more lemon sherbets, just like **BAD NANA** would have, and explained my excellent PLAN. Even Georgina was impressed. We all agreed that while it

was a pretty **risky** PLAN, with **BAD NANA** and Bobby Trulove acting so BADLY and the **variety** of the WINTER WONDERLAND VARIETY SHOW at stake, we ALL had to be super brave . . .

AND GO FOR IT.

Everyone agreed to meet at my house the next day at 7am SHARP!

The Snow Must Go On

The next day was actually the weekend, which was a NICE surprise as what with all the show business and SNOW DAYS I had completely forgotten what day of the week it was. The snow had snowed ALL night and the NEXT morning. It was like someone had rubbed out everybody's footprints from the day before

and everything was twinkly but in a NICE way, not a headachy, sequinny way.

These were COMPLETELY perfect conditions for my plan and I was so excited, but also a bit SCARED, so I couldn't even stay STILL for a single second. I went to Mum and Dad's room, and while he was still half asleep I got Dad to agree to take Marcy, Wilf and me and Jack and even Georgina out on show-business BUSINESS. Once he agreed I then had to actually wake him up properly, which proved very HARD as it was the weekend, but through a combination of winding the clocks *FORWARD* and sending Jack in with some slime, I got him UP and DRESSED in no time!

Marcy, Wilf and even Georgina arrived at 7am SHARP (which Dad thought was 9am because of the clock-winding – I am a genius) and we all had a little huddle round the snowman from the other morning so I could remind them of the plan. Then we all solemnly swore on the snowman that we would do our VERY best and NOT ever snitch and be VERY brave because the WINTER WONDERLAND VARIETY SHOW depended on US and we would NOT let it down! Then it was time for *ACTION* . . .

First of all we got Dad to take us to **BAD NANA'S** and we told him we just had to pop in and ask her about some showbiz stuff. I thought this would be TRICKY as he would want to come in too, but Dad was super happy to just wait outside, and he just sat on the wall (after he had brushed the snow off, obviously, or it would have looked like he'd wet himself and been cold and very soggy). Then we tiptoed up to all the windows and packed snow on to them as HIGH as we could, which was *quite* HIGH when one of you was on all fours and the other was standing on their back.

There was a hairy moment, literally, as *Liberace* started to meow when he saw me (I am almost Dr Dolittle), but I *quickly*

packed the snow up in FRONT of my face, so he COULDN'T see me and he STOPPED meowing. Pheeeow.

Once we had finished packing up BAD NANA'S windows with snow I SUPER casually asked Dad if he would take us to Bobby's because we also needed to ask him some sequin-related questions too. Dad looked like he wasn't that keen and started to talk in that way grown-ups do when they are about to take aaaaaages to say NO to something because they think that if they take aaaaaages you will be TOO bored to argue. Which of course you AREN'T.

This made me slightly start to panic as for one thing Dad might talk for hours, which was time we did NOT have, and for another thing we realllllllly needed him to take us to Bobby's as it's across the BIG road and none of us are allowed to cross it without a grown-up. I was wracking my brains for an IDEA when all of a sudden I heard a whining noise. Well, I immediately looked at Jack because he is usually the source of ALL whining noises.

But it WASN'T him.

It was in fact Georgina, and her whining turned into a cry, and I could have sworn she squeezed out an ACTUAL tear. Well, Dad had NO choice but to take us then. As he led the way, I smiled at Georgina, who even ACTUALLY smiled back and I thought HOW NICE it would be if it was always like this.

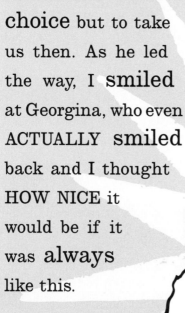

When we got to Bobby Trulove's house, Dad was **more** than happy, again, NOT to get involved in our **show-business** BUSINESS and parked himself on the wall. He **forgot** to brush it down this time so DID actually end up looking like he'd **wet** himself. While he was trying to **dry** his trousers with a used tissue, we got busy packing all the **snow** up against Bobby's windows, just

like we had at **BAD NANA'S**. It was EVEN
easier than **BAD NANA'S** as each window
was made up of loads of ᴛɪɴʏ windows,
which held the snow brilliantly.

After all that, we got Dad to take us to the hall, and no one needed to **pretend** to **cry** because it's next to the paper shop, which Dad **loves**. Once we were in the hall, I used some of my saved-up **sweet money** on the pay phone to call **BAD NANA** and then *Bobby Trulove* to tell them the **snow** had been EXTRA **snowy** that night and NOT to even TRY to **leave** the house as it could be VERY **dangerous** and they couldn't possibly hurt themselves as they were so **important** now, what with the show being THAT actual night and them being at least ninety per cent of the show. As soon as we had **dug** ourselves OUT we would come and **dig** them OUT and it would all be fine and probably best to **rest** up

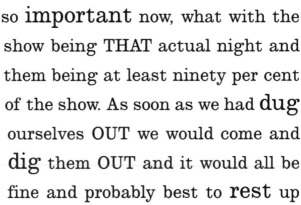

and polish their sequins before the BIG
night really. I did feel BAD about fibbing
and it did actually make me turn a bit
pink, but as I was fibbing on the phone
neither BAD NANA nor Bobby Trulove could
see me going a bit pink, so they just
believed me, which made
me feel WORSE and turn
a bit pinker.

I *knew* my plan was a GOOD plan, but even I was surprised that no one seemed to even *slightly* think we might be up to something. Marcy, Wilf and me and Jack and even Georgina huddled by the stage to CHECK on how our plan was going and we ALL agreed it was going surprisingly well. But we ALL also

agreed that we had quite a way to go so we needed to stay focused. I handed out lemon sherbets to help and realised I was basically being BAD NANA – but before she went razzle-dazzle CRAZY – and that made me feel quite a bit great.

When Mrs Valentine arrived at the hall, she had pink wafer crumbs round her mouth. I was a little SHOCKED as it was ONLY 7.45am (although Dad still thought it was 9.45am) and unless those

crumbs were from the night before I was worried she might be overdoing the pink wafers. But I couldn't let that distract me so we got on with telling her that BAD NANA and Bobby Trulove were STRUCK DOWN with colds and that they would probably NOT be able to make it to the show after all, but that she DIDN'T need to panic.

Well, at this point we had to take a short break to let Mrs Valentine have a LITTLE bit of a panic, but once she had calmed down (and Wilf found her a pink wafer) we told her that it was ALL fine as all the other acts could come back. And without BAD NANA and Bobby Trulove being quite so razzle-dazzle CRAZY they might all want to stay this time and actually be IN the show.

This seemed to calm Mrs Valentine down a bit more and she *even* STOPPED whimpering, which I took as a good SIGN. Then we all trudged through the twinkly snow to round everyone up and to find the missing hula hoops (Wilf found them eventually, round the back of the hall, hidden behind the Brownies' shed) . . . and to get this WINTER WONDERLAND VARIETY SHOW back on the road!

SNOW WAY

Stardust

1 TODAY

AT LEAST **100%**

GeT tHE
SHOW
ON tHE
ROAd

HO!
HO!
HO!

Slowly but surely ALL the acts arrived back. To start with they looked a little **unsure**, but once *Cynth* had got the tea urn on and offered some biscuits around everyone started to look happy and even maybe a bit **excited** about being back in the show. Mrs Valentine still had **BAD NANA'S** air horn and used it to get things started. What with her out the front and Marcy,

Wilf and me and *even* Georgina making sure everything and everyone was where they should be backstage, it was all going really rather well. Even Jack was *slightly* helpful, which was amazing as I have never seen him be anything other than COMPLETELY unhelpful before.

THE WINTER WONDERLAND VARIETY SHOW

really WAS starting to be quite wonderful. The ~~Hooper Doopers~~ had their hoops back, Mr Pickles and Pepé were together again, TINY Daniel Pauls WASN'T crying any more and Penny Heard had even incorporated some KNEE cymbals into her nose-recorder musical recital. Everything started to

THE HOOPER DOOPERS!

MR PICKLES AND PEPE!

TINY DANIEL PAULS!

PENNY HEARD!

(WITH ADDED FOOT CYMBALS)

feel **twinkly** and **exciting** again and
that was really, **really GREAT** until . . .

. . . the hall doors **swung** open and quite **surprisingly** there was **BAD NANA** and *Bobby Trulove*. They looked quite a lot LESS show-businessy than they had been looking that week, and quite a LOT more CROSS and a TEENSY bit soggy, but mainly CROSS. This was confirmed when they stomped over to Mrs Valentine. Marcy, Wilf and me and Jack and even Georgina *RAN* over as *FAST* as our legs would go because we could see Mrs Valentine looking EXTREMELY confused and *quite* a bit scared and we KNEW we had some explaining to do.

Once **BAD NANA** had wrung out her cape and Bobby had dusted down his fancy BIG hat, they STARTED shouting and it didn't seem like they would ever STOP. I think I even saw steam coming off all their wet clothes because they were getting extremely HOT and *quite* a bit bothered. I knew I had to say something to explain why I had done a **BAD NANA**-TYPE trick on actual **BAD NANA**, but they were both getting very SHOUTY and didn't seem to be pausing for breath, which left me with NO room to get a word in. So I had NO choice but to BLAST the air horn. Everyone froze again and I knew I had to say something *quickly*, before they UNfroze, but I was feeling so EXTREMELY worried as I had NEVER had a falling-out with **BAD NANA** before, and while I knew that **usually** she would **agree** with me about ALL this, she WASN'T being at ALL usual.

I took a **deep breath** to try to STOP the butterflies in my tummy from BASHING about and then I said sorry, because I REALLY was. Then I explained that I would rather NOT have had to pile snow up against their windows and pretend they had been snowed in and have to tell them ACTUAL fibs, but they HADN'T left me with much choice. I explained that ever since the WINTER WONDERLAND VARIETY SHOW auditions they had both got more and more razzle-dazzle CRAZY. It had STOPPED them being at all nice and they ONLY seemed interested in being ONSTAGE for as long as possible. I said THAT was a shame because while they were very good at being onstage, other people in our town were good TOO, and it would be sad NOT to see everyone, and anyway you can have TOO much of a good thing. AND when it came down to it, it was called a VARIETY show and while there were two of them I didn't really think THAT was much of a variety.

Once I STOPPED talking my butterflies started BASHING about again and I tried to do a winning smile, but I don't think I managed it. BAD NANA and Bobby Trulove looked at each other and then at me and I did a little wobble because I had NO idea what was going

N⁰.1 SMILER?

to happen. And then **BAD NANA** looked just like Jack did when Mum caught him RED-HANDED eating my birthday cake the day before my trampolining party (literally, it was covered in RED icing) and Bobby looked down at his sequin jazz shoes and then sort of mumbled something. Cynth said they would have to speak up because NO ONE could hear them. Then they just mumbled a bit LOUDER so we could hear the mumbling better, but still couldn't work out what the WORDS were. Then Mrs Valentine said she was sorry but she STILL couldn't understand what they were saying and then they mumbled even louder. And then Mr Pickles said, "Pardon?" and they both shouted SORRY at the same time.

BAD NANA explained that they really were sorry and they could see now that they had got a bit dazzled by the razzle and the dazzle and that sometimes when you are OLD, people don't think you can DO anything let alone show business so it was just NICE to do something you were good at, but that was NO EXCUSE and they did get carried away and they really DIDN'T want to hurt people's feelings and SORRY. Then Bobby Trulove said same from him.

I wasn't really sure what to do next. I tried to make my face look like Mum's does when she has just told me off, sort of worried but still a bit cross. I'm not sure I managed it, so I gave up and gave BAD NANA a BIG hug instead and it was so COMPLETELY brilliant, except for it being a little bit soggy.

Then Jack pressed the AIR HORN and we all froze again and he pointed out that it was getting LATE and the show was THAT actual night and we needed to get a wiggle on and UNBELIEVABLY, because he is ALWAYS wrong,

HE
WAS
RIGHT.

HAPPY
DAYS

Super
Star

Well, everyone went BONKERS rehearsing and making the set and drinking tea and eating biscuits. Even the WI turned up to HELP us paint scenery and they offered us their biscuits too. Dad made one of his usual unfunny jokes about wanting to get BACK to WORK for a rest and Mum even came down with sandwiches for everyone and NONE of them were fish paste. It was really nice that the WINTER WONDERLAND VARIETY SHOW was fun again and for everyone again and had variety again.

Marcy, Wilf and me and Jack realised we had been so busy we hadn't had

any time to **practise** our act, but **BAD NANA** said maybe we could ALL do a turn together, with Bobby, if we liked. And it turned out we DID like, so we ALL had a little **practice** and it WASN'T perfect or *even* that sequinny but it WAS fun and I couldn't wait.

When we had finished the set and decorations, and hung up about a BILLION fairy lights, the stage with the ~~swishy red curtains~~ looked REALLY fancy.

I asked Bobby if it looked
as fancy as the fancy ones
he used to tread on and he
said EVEN fancier, and we
ALL felt DOUBLE proud.

Well, after EVERYTHING that had already happened that day the actual show wasn't even that nervous-making. Everyone who wasn't IN the show seemed to have come to watch it and although Mrs Valentine did look *quite* scared, once the music started and the lights went on and the Hooper Doopers started hooping, there was NOTHING else to do but keep going, really.

When it was our turn and our act went **wrong** LOTS and LOTS of times, it turned out Georgina was **right** – it was

pretty funny. But we were laughing TOO, so we were fine with that.

All in all, **everyone** AGREED that
the WINTER WONDERLAND VARIETY SHOW was
a **wonderful** wintery SUCCESS and
certainly did have LOTS and LOTS of
variety and even *Liberace* got in on
the finale.

As we all stood onstage and enjoyed our
applause, **BAD NANA** whispered to me that

she really was sorry and **promised** never to go razzle-dazzle CRAZY again and that she was so **super duper** PROUD of ME and my **plan** and that it was the **best** plan ever. And, while APPLAUSE is very **nice**, *that* actually felt like the **best** thing **ever** and I really thought I might BURST right **there** and **then**.

And just like THAT, all of a sudden, after everything . . . it was OVER and everyone walked through the snow back to **BAD NANA'S**. And she finally made those fancy hot chocolates with ALL the trimmings she'd promised us.

I said that it had all been very exciting and while I was glad the show had gone really well and everyone had enjoyed it, now I felt a bit sad it was all OVER

and even slightly missed the twinkles. And then **BAD NANA** said, "Well, THAT'S show business," and Wilf said didn't she mean SNOW business and then I laughed so much hot chocolate came OUT of my nose.

As I snuggled down in bed that night,
I realised a few things . . .

1. Even though they might
not LOOK like it, old people
have still got razzle and
dazzle, and sometimes they
even have TOO much.

2. Snow is
the BEST thing
ever.

3. Now that hot chocolate
has come OUT of my nose
it will NEVER taste the
same and I MUSTN'T drink
nice drinks around
Wilf any more.

4. Sometimes
grown-ups
get overexcited
TOO.

5. When I am a bit **bigger**, I might want to be a *hula-hooper* instead of a *twirler.*

6. Even **BAD NANA** can get it a BIT **wrong** sometimes . . .

But, when she DOES,
she gets it WRONG in
sequins!

HAVE YOU READ...

Sophy Henn

BAD Nana

OLDER NOT WISER

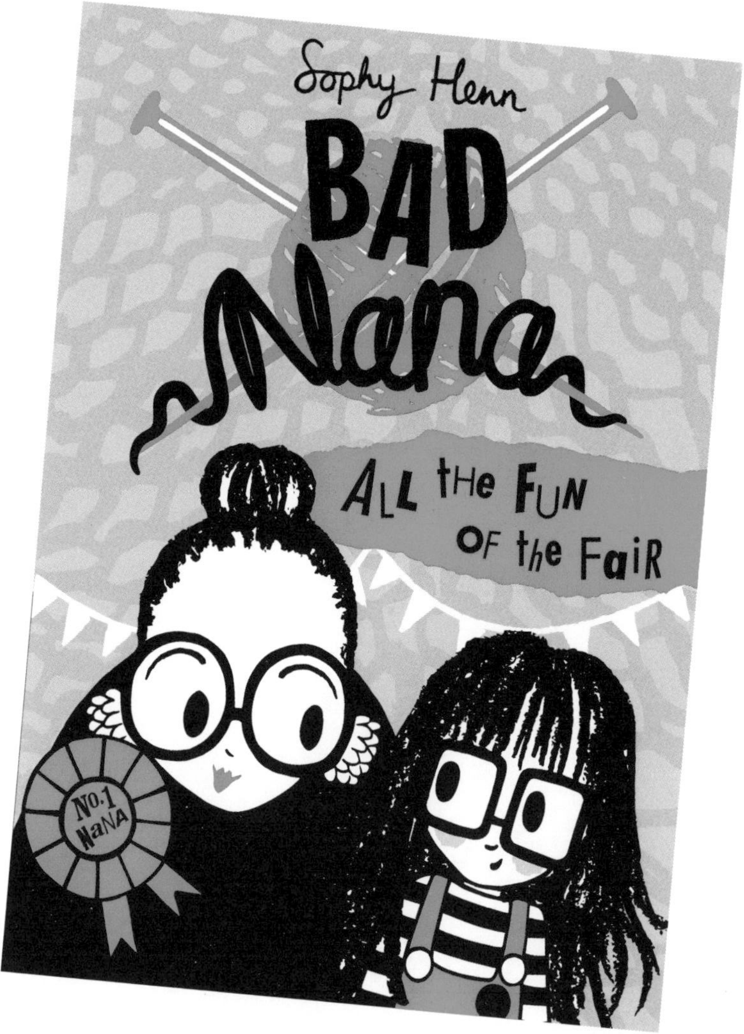

So bad SHE'S Good